MW00761639

TALL TALES of JENNY GOLD

by Sue LaNeve

ROURKE
Educational Media
rourkeeducationalmedia.com

© 2017 Rourke Educational Media

All rights reserved. No part of this book may be reproduced or utilized in any form or by any means, electronic or mechanical including photocopying, recording, or by any information storage and retrieval system without permission in writing from the publisher.

www.rourkeeducationalmedia.com

Edited by: Keli Sipperley
Cover layout by: Rhea Magaro
Interior layout by: Jen Thomas
Cover Illustration by: Giuliano Aloisi

Library of Congress PCN Data

Tall Tales of Jenny Gold / Sue LaNeve
 (History Files)
 ISBN (hard cover)(alk. paper) 978-1-68191-678-1
 ISBN (soft cover) 978-1-68191-779-5
 ISBN (e-Book) 978-1-68191-879-2
 Library of Congress Control Number: 2016932555

Printed in the United States of America,
North Mankato, Minnesota

Dear Parents and Teachers,

The History Files series takes readers into significant eras in United States history, allowing them to walk in the shoes of characters living in the periods they've learned about in the classroom. From the journey to a new beginning on the Mayflower, to the strife of the Vietnam War and beyond, each title in this series delves into the experiences of diverse characters struggling with the conflicts of their time.

Each book includes a comprehensive summary of the era, along with background information on the real people that the fictional characters mention or encounter in the novel. Additional websites to visit and an interview with the author are also included.

In addition, each title is supplemented with online teacher/parent notes with ideas for incorporating the book into a lesson plan. These notes include subject matter, background information, inspiration for maker space activities, comprehension questions, and additional online resources. Notes are available at: www.RourkeEducationalMedia.com.

We hope you enjoy the History Files books as much as we do.

Happy reading,
Rourke Educational Media

Table of Contents

Chapter One
How Did I End Up in this Place?

The first thing Jenny Gold hated about her new bedroom was the color: mustard. It reminded her of throw-up sprinkled with amber dust. The rest of the room appeared fairly normal: beds, a dresser, and an old mahogany rocking chair.

The chair sat next to a small window, and a medium-sized wooden box sat next to the chair. Her mother's fancy black and rose Chanel scarf adorned the top of the box. And atop of the scarf-covered wooden box sat a kerosene lamp that Cora and Leo provided.

Jenny's daddy kept a watchful eye on the room. More exactly, he looked out from inside his framed photograph that leaned against the mirror on the dresser. Reuben's comb, Mother's hairpins, and Jenny's brush lay atop a lace doily next to it. Those particular items explain the second thing Jenny hated about the room: She shared it with her younger brother Reuben, and their mother.

Most days, Jenny's feelings about moving to Leo and Cora's farm rumbled and roared like a train speeding inside her body. Sometimes she spat them out at Mother. Otherwise, her brain would get foggy. It had been doing that since her old life in New York City collapsed.

Jenny stared out the small bedroom window at Reuben, who hung from a branch in the lone tree that shaded the house. Her mother had just turned up the dirt path to the barn, her legs pumping the pedals of the bike Leo had given her for work.

Jenny rolled her eyes. Mother had never worked before. Or ridden a bike for that matter. At least not that she could remember. Mother leaned the bike against the tree and wiped the dust from her work pants. In a flash, Reuben dropped to the ground, and Jenny jumped on the bed to stretch out. No sense wasting an opportunity to show how tough her own day had been.

Once inside, Mother placed the cloth bag

Cora had given her on a peg by the door. Behind the cloth bag hung the only designer purse she still owned. Cora had said, "If you're going to work at the general store, you best take a more practical purse."

Jenny rolled on her side. Through slit eyes she watched Reuben lead Mother to the rocking chair. He bent over slightly at the waist, and spread his arm out as if to say, "Your majesty, your chair."

Mother hugged his head and tussled his hair. "Hello my darlings," she said. Jenny closed her eyes tightly when Mother looked her way, but didn't miss a word. "Did you know it's absolutely true what they say about riding a bike?" Mother asked.

"What's true?" Reuben replied.

Something smacked Jenny in the head. She sprung upright to see a pillow in her lap and Reuben giggling. "Reuben!"

"Please, please be careful, dear." Mother leaned back in the rocker. "To answer your question, you never forget how to ride a bike. It's quite a distance to town."

Jenny's interest suddenly multiplied. "How far?" she asked. The possibility of going to town, of going shopping someday, lifted her spirits.

"No idea. On the bright side, I shall have strong muscles in no time. Now tell me about your day."

Jenny slid her legs over the side of the bed. "What's there to tell, Mother? Cora makes me work till my knuckles are torn up like a farmer's. I'm nearly thirteen, but my hands look ancient." Jenny spread her fingers wide to display the nicks and rough fingernails. "And you should hear her go on and on about this farm as if it were Saks Fifth Avenue."

"Try to be kind, Jenny," Mother said, her voice growing weary.

But in her best imitation of Cora's voice, Jenny warbled, "My ancestor's blood, sweat, and tears went into this farm."

Reuben couldn't hold in his giggles. He kneeled to untie Mother's work shoes. Warbling his voice as best he could, he added, "And I've walked every inch of this property."

"My darlings," Mother said, and laughed, unable to hold it in. She put her stockinged feet up on the bed. "Leo and Cora have given us a home for a while and we must show our appreciation."

"It sure isn't the life Daddy wanted for us," Jenny said.

"Please, dear heart, don't say that," Mother whispered, her eyes welling up.

Jenny looked toward his photo on the dresser. "I just miss him so much."

"Me too," Reuben said, plopping down on his bed.

"Do you know what Cora told me?" Jenny asked, changing the subject. She reached over to nudge Reuben's shoulder. "She said, 'Bring in all the eggs without breaking a one, clean the chicken coop, and milk the cows. Do that promptly and I won't make you scrub the outhouse.' " Jenny sighed and shook her head. "Can you imagine scrubbing the outhouse? That would be horrid! I simply could not do it."

Reuben grabbed another pillow. "Don't you touch me with those chicken poop, outhouse hands!" he said, and pulled the pillow up to his mouth to hold back more giggles. Then he flung it at Jenny.

"I'll get you good and smelly," she said, and popped the pillow up in the air, then smacked it back at Reuben, knocking over the kerosene lamp that sat on the box.

Mother grabbed it as it grazed her leg. "Thank goodness this wasn't lit. You two must stop this." She set the lamp on the floor and lifted her scarf off the box to inspect it.

Jenny slid off the bed, stubbing her toe on the box, which she'd thought was empty. She kneeled down and ran her fingers along an edge. "What's inside of this?" she said, lifting the lid off.

"A few surprises I was saving for you."

Reuben kneeled next to her and watched as Jenny removed wadded up balls of newspaper. "Let me see, let me see," he said. "Oh look, Mother! My Lincoln Logs. And my Spirit of St. Louis!"

"I thought you'd sold everything," Jenny said. She lifted the container of wooden logs and Reuben's prized model plane out of the box and carefully placed them on the floor. "Please tell me you packed something for me," Jenny said, pulling out more balls of paper.

Mother's eyes had closed. "You'll see," she said.

Nestled in more newspaper, Jenny found a small velvet bag that held her old jacks and ball set and Tiddlywinks game. Moving more paper aside, her breath caught in her throat.

"What is it?" Reuben asked, his hand flying the Spirit of St. Louis past her face.

"The diary Daddy gave me," Jenny said.

Reuben teared up. "That was a long time ago."

Jenny pointed at her mother, whose breathing sounded like she'd slipped into a deep sleep. She whispered, "That Mr. Hilbig works Mother so hard at his grocery store." Reuben nodded, and held a finger up to his mouth.

Jenny collected her treasures and placed the jacks and Tiddlywinks on the dresser, next to Daddy's photograph. She cradled the diary in her hands and looked again out the window. Her diary held memories of her old life. A life so different than this one on the farm.

Reuben's tap on her shoulder brought her back. He pointed to the Lincoln Logs he'd spread on the floor. "Want to play?" he whispered.

"Sorry. Maybe later." Jenny carried the diary back to her bed. She curled up on her side and opened the small book to the first entry. The date at the top of the page was October 8, 1929. *Almost two years ago*, she thought. Her mind went back to her old bedroom in their beautiful brownstone home on a tree-lined street in New York City. October 8, 1929. The beginning of the end.

Chapter Two
The Diary

~~~~~~~~~~

BEFORE: Manhattan Brownstone, New York, New York

October 8, 1929
Dear Diary,

This is my very first letter to you. I have never owned a diary before. How shall I begin? Yesterday was Daddy's birthday. It was a glorious evening for Reuben and me.

Right before dinner, Mother lit the candles on Daddy's birthday cake. We sang Happy Birthday, and Daddy gave each of us a present! Then he said what he always says. "I want for nothing, meine Kinder. You are my birthday presents."

Reuben got a new Lincoln Log set to add to his old one. Now he can make even grander cabins. And Daddy gave me this diary! It's a much more grown-up present than last year's doll. Oh, but she was wonderful. She stood as tall as me, had curly brown hair and big brown eyes just like mine. She even said, "Ma Ma!" I named her Mary. You must remember Mary Brian, dear diary! My favorite star in that old Peter Pan movie before talkies?

Daddy laughed when Reuben and I surprised him with a fishing rod! Like Mother said, now maybe he'll get out of his stuffy old bank office.

We had the happiest dinner. Lupe set the table with Mother's finest linen and silver, and cooked Daddy's favorite brisket. Afterward, Reuben and I snuck icing off Daddy's birthday cake before Mother cut us each a slice. I think I will sneak down later for some more!

Well, that's all for now, dear diary. Oh, I almost forgot! Yesterday, Lupe brought her granddaughter Dolly with her when she came to clean. No matter what Mother says, Dolly is such fun to play with. I like her very much. We played Tiddlywinks until we heard Mother coming. Then, ha ha, we played hide and seek.

PS: I think I'm going to like talking to you.

⌒⌒⌒⌒⌒⌒⌒⌒⌒⌒⌒

Tuesday, October 22, 1929
Dear Diary,

I hate school very much. Today, ole Miss Billygoat called me up to the chalkboard. I'd been so busy telling Mona Talbert about what Dolly and I found. How was I supposed to solve that silly multiplication problem? Miss Billygoat said, "Jenny, dear, you're not paying attention in class. I've given you two warnings. Now march yourself down to the headmaster's office." Well, when I told Mr. Z what I just told you, he took a yardstick and slapped me across my bottom, he did. I haven't told Mother yet. She'll be so mad at me for getting in trouble again. Maybe if I show her the magical coin Dolly and I found in the attic, she'll forgive me.

PS: Dolly comes over with Lupe every few days. We're getting to be good friends.

⌒⌒⌒⌒⌒⌒⌒⌒⌒⌒⌒

Thursday, October 24, 1929
Dear Diary,

   Daddy worked late tonight. Lupe fixed us eggs for dinner. Yuck. Reuben and I were doing our homework when Daddy arrived. His skin looked as gray as a raincloud. I think he must be getting the plague. I caught him and Mother whispering. Then Mother sent Reuben and me up to our rooms, but she was wearing that smile she always wears when she has a wonderful secret. Like that night she and Daddy woke us up very late to go on a vacation. Maybe they are planning a surprise for us when Daddy feels better.

   But I have a secret too! I never told Mother about the gold coin. Dolly and I think it might be magical. Well, finders keepers, losers weepers, I always say. Besides, Mother walloped me good and won't let me listen to the Children's Hour for a month! All because of that horrible Miss Billygoat. Well, maybe I should "turn a new leaf" like Mother said and call Mrs. Billygoat by her real name. Bahhh. Bahhh.

PS: Dolly and I did our homework together. She helped me with my division problems. She is so smart!

PPS: We played hide and seek with the gold coin. Before Dolly comes back to see me, I have to find where she hid it.

☙☙☙☙☙☙☙☙☙☙

Friday, October 25, 1929
Dear Diary,

Like always, Daddy walked me and Reuben to school on his way to the bank. Reuben was chattering away about that Lindbergh fellow. "I want to become a pilot, too, Daddy," he'd said, "and fly all by myself across the ocean." Well, Daddy said, "That's nice, Reuben." But dear diary, I don't believe he was paying any attention to him. And today, Mother had been listening to the radio when Daddy came home from work. He snapped at her! "We won't be listening to this anymore!" he said, and took it upstairs to his bedroom!

PS: Mother must have told him about me

getting in trouble at school. See what you've started, Miss Billygoat?

☙☙☙☙☙☙☙☙☙☙

November 13, 1929
Dear Diary,

I'm sorry I haven't written you in nearly three weeks. Something has been very wrong. Mother keeps saying, "Daddy's having trouble at work." But he never talks about work in front of us so she won't say why. After dinner last night, Reuben came in my room crying. He said it felt like the day Baubie and Zadie were in that accident. Like they died all over again.

Then, a wonderful thing happened. Daddy tucked me in bed, and said, "Tomorrow night is the symphony, Jenny. Sleep tight." I said, "We're not going to have to sell all our tickets?" He seemed surprised. "Have you been eavesdropping?" he asked, and pinched both of my cheeks like he always does. When I told him I'd overhead Mother talking on the phone, he said, "Music feeds the soul, my

19

darling. We will never sell our tickets." Oh dear diary, I think things might be all right after all.

Well, I expected to go shopping for new clothes after school today, the way we always do before the symphony. But instead, Mother said we were to have a fashion show. "We'll use these clothes from your closet." I put on one of my old things, and Mother said, "This dress will work perfectly." Reuben's trousers were so short, his ankles would have caught a cold. Mother laughed and I thought for sure she would change her mind and take us on a fun shopping trip. Instead, she took the thread out of the hem, and didn't even wait for Lupe to iron them. I didn't know Mother knew how to iron. Or sew. But that's just what she did.

If I get ink on my dress, she'll have to buy me a new one. I could use my gold coin, but Dolly and I are having fun playing hide and seek with it. It's her turn to find it.

PS: Lupe stopped coming to our house every day. Dolly said my mother can only afford to pay her once a week.

PPS: What is going on? Are we poor all of a sudden?

☙☙☙☙☙☙☙☙☙☙☙

NOW: The Farmhouse in Crossroads, Colorado, 1931

"Jenny? It's time to fix dinner."

Jenny closed her diary, thinking what a foolish girl she had been back in New York. New clothes? The symphony? She headed to the kitchen.

In her warbled voice, Cora said, "You picked some fine ears of corn today, Jenny. Clean those up for dinner. I'm roasting a chicken."

Living on a farm surely improved one aspect of life. During those last weeks in New York, Mother had to sell things to buy food. But as Jenny shucked an ear of corn, her memories went further back, to when Lupe used to shop for all of their groceries and prepare all of their meals. Oh how she missed Lupe. And Dolly too.

Jenny put on an apron the way Cora had instructed to protect her clothes. Since she helped wash clothes, this actually made sense to her. Cora looked up from picking pin feathers off the chicken. "Your hard work paid off, Jenny. Mr. Hilbig gave Leo and I twenty cents a dozen for the eggs you collected."

"Well, I sure hope he has enough money left to pay Mother. She's working so hard."

"If she does her work, he'll pay her. Mr. Hilbig is a generous and honest man." Cora nodded toward the huge kitchen table. "And when you're done with that corn, I'll need you to put those things in the pantry."

Jenny looked behind her. Large bags made out of pretty flowered fabric were piled on the table. "Where did all that come from?" she asked, carrying the corn husks to throw into the compost barrel outside.

"The money Mr. Hilbig paid us for the eggs allowed us to fill our pantry. It's the way of the farm. And now you're part of it."

Ugh, Jenny thought. *I'm a farmer?* She

cleared the table, putting the sacks full of flour, sugar, and coffee into the pantry. "Cora, this flour sack looks a lot like your dress. Did your dressmaker buy the same fabric?" she said.

"My dressmaker? You are a funny girl. I sew my own clothes, thank you very much. Those cotton flour and sugar sacks make fine material when money is tight."

"Flour sack dresses?" Jenny could hardly believe her ears.

"Best remember times are tough, Jenny," she said. "Like they say, 'Repair, reuse, make do, and don't throw anything away.'"

Jenny carried the container of kerosene for their lamps out to the storm porch. Another wave of sadness stunned her. *A farmer? Would Daddy approve of this?*

Like every night before dinner, she set the table. But tonight she replayed the events of Daddy's wonderful birthday dinner. The napkins Cora had sewn turned into fine white linen, the old plates into delicate china. Her daydream turned the old farm table into one dressed with sparkling crystal and shiny sterling silverware that Lupe had set. Oh how she missed Dolly and Lupe and her old life. But mainly she missed Daddy.

ᚑᚑᚑᚑᚑᚑᚑᚑᚑᚑ

Jenny's new "family" ate the roasted chicken, corn, cut tomatoes, fresh bread and churned butter. The whole while, Jenny couldn't wait to get back to her diary. But first, there was dough to make and knead.

Cora had taught her how to make bread. On even nights, Cora made loaves. On odd nights, like tonight, it was Jenny's turn.

When they'd first arrived at the farm, Jenny felt like arguing about most everything—sharing a room, wearing old clothes every day. No radio. No music. Outhouses. Chicken poop. But kneading the dough relaxed her. She began looking forward to it, to the smells of bread baking.

Before bed, she and Reuben headed out to the little building that stood next to a fence. Inside, the outhouse toilet looked like a large box with a round hole cut into the top. It emptied into a deep well below. At first, Jenny and Reuben had laughed at the idea of using an outdoor bathroom. Reuben grew to like it though, especially when he was playing outside. Jenny still hated it, always imagining falling through the hole.

Reuben headed back to the house to give her some privacy. She stared at the wooden walls, almost in a trance. Her whole body startled when something tickled her leg. "No, no, no!" she cried out after realizing it was a spider. She jumped off the box, wondering what might crawl up through the opening.

Later, as she heated water on the stove, she daydreamed about her tub in New York, and how they used to bathe every night. Here, it wasn't her turn to take a bath until Sunday. Still, Mother made her and Reuben use a cloth and a washbowl full of warm water to freshen up before bed.

With her diary in hand, Jenny was finally able to curl up in the chair next to the kerosene lamp. Mother tucked Reuben in bed, then placed her hairpins on the dresser and brushed her hair. She kissed Daddy's face through the glass in the frame. Jenny felt a kiss on the top of her head right before Mother collapsed in their bed. "Tomorrow we will go through your clothes to see what you will need for school."

"School?" Jenny's eyes grew large enough to take in the enormity of what Mother had just said. She'd been too busy with farm work to even think about school. She wouldn't know anyone. There was no money for new clothes. And she'd have to make up more stories—fancy ones—about her family, and why they'd moved to Colorado. Tall tales like she'd told her friends back in New York. In that moment, Jenny decided she'd simply skip a year of school until things got better.

She opened her diary and lost herself in its pages.

BEFORE: Manhattan Brownstone, New York, New York

November 15, 1929
Dear Diary,

I love, love, love the symphony and I love "Bolero" even more! It's mostly all solos—first a drummer, then a man playing a flute, then one playing a clarinet, then a bassoon, then a clarinet, an oboe, and a saxophone. Each musician played the same notes, one instrument after the other. You'd think it'd get boring. But it didn't. I felt like I was in a magical trance or on a magic carpet. At the end, they all played the music together. Mr. Ravel must have been so happy when the audience stood up and clapped.

PS: I asked Daddy if we could buy the album. That got a smile out of him. "Someday," he said.

January 10, 1930
Dear Diary,

Hope you didn't miss me too much. Daddy snapped at Mother again today. We've had no happy celebrations. No special presents. We had chicken for Thanksgiving. And then a couple days before the first night of Chanukah, Mother said, "My darlings, these are difficult times and there is joy in giving. This year, let's go through our belongings. Surely, we'll find things we can give to those less fortunate than we are." I thought it was a wonderful idea to make room for our new presents. Well guess what? That's not what she meant. Instead of getting anything, we're giving our old clothes and toys away.

At school, Trudy Ecklestein and Mona Talbert showed off their wonderful new sweaters, and both of them had gotten new necklaces from their dads. They looked at me like I was a rutabaga. Trudy said, "Everything okay at home, Jenny?" Well, I told them what Mother told us, about giving instead of getting because of how blessed we were. They seemed impressed. Or at least they acted normal again.

Everything about life was feeling a bit dark. Then today, Mother flipped the light switch. First, she surprised Reuben and me after school, carrying bags full of wonderful new clothes and something called a yoyo! Dear diary, it's the bee's knees! Really tricky, but so fun to play with. Of course, Reuben figured it out right away. The best part of today is that she bought tickets to Chasing Rainbows *tomorrow night! My first talkie! Oh, I hope it cheers up Daddy! But Mother said to keep it a surprise.*

PS: Mother bought the "Bolero" record album too!

PPS: I sure hope the lights stay on for a while.

ᘒᘒᘒᘒᘒᘒᘒᘒᘒᘒᘒ

February 1, 1930
Dear Diary,

Daddy yelled at Mother! Really yelled! "You aren't listening to me!" he said, and left the room still yelling, and madder than I've ever seen him. "Movie tickets? We can't do things like this anymore!" I couldn't breathe. He made Reuben cry. Mother said she had to help Daddy in the kitchen. Daddy came back smiling. Said he was sorry, bad day. After dinner, I heard him say, "I'm so sorry. It is my job to provide for us."

On our way home from the movie, Daddy kept humming one of its songs, "Happy Days Are Here Again." He even twirled Mother in circles as we walked.

When we got home, he put "Bolero" on our Victor and pretended to be the conductor. As each new musical instrument began to play its solo, Daddy pointed his imaginary baton at me and I named the instrument.

PS: Chasing Rainbows was glorious. I didn't have to read what the actors were saying.

PPS: Guess what Mother did to make all of this happiness happen? She sold one of her fancy rings.

Chapter Three
A House of Cards

⌒⌒⌒⌒⌒⌒⌒⌒⌒⌒

NOW: A Farmhouse in Crossroads, Colorado, 1931

Jenny groaned when the rooster crowed. She got up and shook Reuben's shoulder. "Rise and shine," she said. The two donned their work clothes and ran outside to collect eggs, milk the cows, and clean the chicken coop.

Hungrier than she'd ever been before, Jenny savored the smoky flavor of ham in her mouth. Cora made buttermilk biscuits. And a neighbor had brought over homemade jam. No matter how much Jenny rejected becoming a farm girl, no matter how much she missed her rich life in New York, she never forgot all those months when they ate nothing but toast for breakfast.

Mother was not on Mr. Helig's schedule at the grocery store today. Back in the family bedroom, she announced, "Fashion show!"

Jenny stared at the photo of Daddy. "Mother, do you remember the night we saw *Chasing Rainbows*?"

"How could I forget? What a wonderful night that was, dancing on the street with your father." When she turned around, Mother's eyes were filled with tears.

Jenny turned and hugged her mother from behind. "I wish we could listen to that music again."

"Me too," Reuben said.

Mother moved the oil lamp to the floor. "Open the treasure box again, Jenny. There are a few more surprises for you."

"I thought I'd emptied the box!" she said, tossing aside balls of newspaper, revealing a familiar record label—the word VICTOR in large letters at the top. Under Victor was an illustration of a dog sitting next to large sound horn on a wind-up Victor phonograph. "You didn't sell them? Oh, thank you, Mother!

Jenny lifted two albums out of the box—Ravel's "Bolero" and the soundtrack from *Chasing Rainbows*.

"Someday," Mother said, nodding for Reuben to try on a pair of pants, "we'll get another Victor, or maybe a Victrola this time."

Jenny returned the records to the box, her frustration rumbling through her chest again. She pulled her diary out from under her bed. It was her last connection to the father she loved so dearly, but hated for leaving them.

BEFORE: Manhattan Brownstone, New York, New York

March 8, 1930
Dear Diary,

Mother says, "Less meat and more beans," because she wants us to be healthy. I said I thought we were eating beans because we're poor all of a sudden. "Poor?" she stared at me for a long time. "We have a home, a loving family and . . ." Well, I stopped listening. I want brisket.

At dinner, I asked Daddy what happened at that cattle auction place. The children in my class said it was collapsing. After he stopped laughing, he explained that the stock market wasn't a cattle place. "It has to do with business. Like mine."

Well, his explanation was so confusing. And since Daddy doesn't talk about work, it made me nervous. Maybe if I write it down it will help.

Businesses sell little pieces of ownership in their company when they need money to pay more people or make new products. The pieces are called shares of stock. In good times, people buy lots of shares. That makes the stock's price go up and helps the business make money.

Well, I guess times are really terrible. Daddy said, "Instead of buying stock, people are selling their shares. That pushes the stock prices down and puts the companies selling stock in trouble. They can't pay their employees. And then those people have to sell even more stock to feed their families and pay their mortgages."

Daddy kept talking and talking. "Now the whole megillah *is falling like a house of cards," he said. "But you and Reuben are growing up." Then he went upstairs to his bedroom and came back with the radio. "It's time for the whole family to understand what's going on in the world."*

Well, President Hoover said the worst of the stock market crash will be over in the next sixty days. He said prosperity was around the corner. I asked Daddy what prosperity meant and he said, "The way we used to live, my darling."

PS: You're not going to believe what Reuben did all night. He sat on the carpeting with a deck of playing cards, trying to figure out how to build a house of cards.

꩜꩜꩜꩜꩜꩜꩜꩜꩜

April 15, 1930
Dear Diary,

I want prosperity back. No new clothes. No new books. Reuben and I may have to go to PS #316 next year, which is kind of scary. I've gone to the Leder Academy my whole life. But at least I won't have to keep coming up with stories to tell Mona Talbert.

PS: I love the library! I checked out Robin Hood and His Merry Men. *Turns out he stole from the rich and gave to the poor. Truly, the money belonged to the poor in the first place. Would he have stolen from my family or given us things?*

PPS: Reuben finally built his house! It's a little building made of playing cards leaning against each other. He kneeled beside it and said, "Watch this!" He blew on the cards and they all came tumbling down.

ᘓᘓᘓᘓᘓᘓᘓᘓᘓᘓ

April 15, 1930
Dear Diary,

Lupe was crying and Mother sent Reuben and me to our rooms. But from the top of the stairs we heard Lupe say, "Your government is making us go back to Mexico . . . we are taking too many jobs from Americans." And then she left.

It's so unfair. Poor Dolly. Does she think we sent them back to Mexico? We never got to say goodbye to each other.

PS: It was my turn to find the gold coin.

෨෨෨෨෨෨෨෨෨

June 22, 1930
Dear Diary,

Reuben said Charles Lindbergh had a baby. Well, HE didn't. But you know what I mean. Daddy says Reuben is an "authority" on the guy. Reuben plans to make friends with the baby and someday they'll fly planes together.

Another shocker. Mother said, "You and Reuben will go to Mr. Dan's beach house by yourselves this summer. Like Daddy said, you're growing up." Mr. Dan is Daddy's best friend from college. My family goes to his beach house every summer.

PS: Truly, I detest sand. But I love how waves make shushing sounds. They're a lot better to listen to than Mother and Daddy's arguments.

PPS: Reuben and I have never been away from Mother and Daddy before.

NOW: A Farmhouse in Crossroads, Colorado, 1931

"Time to put the diary down, Jenny. It's your turn!" When Jenny looked up, Mother was resting her arms atop Reuben's clothes, piled high in her lap. She sighed. "I will simply have to let out seams and lengthen the hems on all of them."

"Like Cora said," Reuben announced in Cora's warbled voice, " 'Make do and mend.' " And with that, he ran outside to help Leo.

As mother sorted Reuben's clothes, Jenny remembered first meeting Leo. "Nice to meet you, New York Jenny," he'd said. "Cora and I are right happy to have you here to help us keep our farm running."

Jenny had watched Leo work with only one farmhand from sunrise to sunset—

bundling hay, carrying corn. Times were tough, all right. People couldn't afford to buy his crops. He had to morgage the farm. And if he missed a payment on his mortgage, some other farm owner might take Cora's land away. So he let go of six farmhands.

"Come on, darling," Mother said, handing Jenny a dress.

After trying on three, Jenny flung herself back on her bed. "Oh, Mother. They're all too short. I must get new clothes!"

Mother leaned forward and pulled down on the hem of the dress. "Did you know fashionable women have been wearing shorter skirts these days?"

Jenny sat up. Her mother knew fashion. Or she'd known it back in New York, when she could afford to buy a new dress every day. "Well, if you say so," Jenny said. "Because I surely do not want to stand out. It will be hard enough starting at a new school. I really think I should just take a year off."

Mother sat next to her on the bed. "You will not be taking anything off except for that dress so I can fix it. And yes, it will be a very different school than what you were used to in the city."

"How do you mean," Jenny said, examining herself in the mirror.

"Well, of course, it's a public school."

"Wonderful."

Mother stared at Jenny's reflection. "They begin the school year late in October so all the children can help with the fall harvest. There are only two rooms in this rural school. One classroom is for children in first through fifth grade and the other is for those in sixth through eighth grade."

"That's horrid. Can't I go back to New York?" Jenny said, even though she knew that was impossible. The idea just seemed better than the unknown.

"And live where, Jenny? Stand up, please. Straight, my darling. Hmm . . . we will have to see about getting you a brassiere soon."

"Mother!" Jenny's eyes darted around the room, to ensure Reuben hadn't snuck back in. Her face had turned as red as the apples on

Cora's trees.

Mother's eyes smiled. "We really can't afford to purchase one, but perhaps I can make you the kind that the flappers have been wearing."

"The flappers? Do they even wear them?" Jenny asked, remembering the girls in those fancy short fringed dresses that looked so different from what other women had been wearing.

"Yes dear. They wear bodices that are simple bands to flatten the chest. I'll be able to sew one for you."

"Fine. If you must. But please do not talk about this in front of Reuben."

"Jenny?" It was Cora, calling her again. "It's time to wash clothes."

Standing at the half-barrel, Jenny pushed the clothes around in the water made sudsy with flakes of Super Suds. She always missed Lupe, but especially on laundry days. Back home, she found clean clothes in her drawers and clean dresses hanging in her closet, as if by magic.

She fed a shirt through two rollers and turned the handle to squeeze out most of the water. Back home, Lupe didn't allow Jenny or Dolly to play in the basement on laundry day. So Jenny never knew how hard Lupe worked.

Outside Cora and Leo were chatting. Jenny didn't mean to eavesdrop, but their voices carried. And what she heard frightened her. Phrases like "The drought is destroying. . ." and "How will we pay for. . ." She heard them say her name and Reuben's name, reminding Jenny of her parents' secret conversations.

By bedtime, Jenny was certain she could fall asleep standing up. But reading her diary had become more than remembering her old life. She'd never found the gold coin Dolly had hidden. Had she written something that would help her remember?

Chapter Four
The Bottom Falls Out

⌒⌒⌒⌒⌒⌒⌒⌒⌒⌒⌒

BEFORE: Manhattan Brownstone, New York, New York

August 30, 1930
Dear Diary,

Should have brought you to Mr. Dan's beach house. Ginger and Mathew may be pretend cousins but they're swell. That's my new word. The first day, Ginger said, "Wait till you see my new bathing suits!" Dear diary, they barely covered the top of her back. And you can see most of her thighs. She is so daring. I said, "I almost got the same one. But Mother made me give it to a girl who begged at our front door." And when Mr. Dan said he missed having Mother and Daddy with us, I told him they were too busy feeding people back in the city. Then Ginger got in trouble for talking about the European vacation they're taking after we left. She treated me differently after that, kind of how Mona and Trudy were acting right before school let out. Worse yet, school starts next week.

PS: Mr. Dan is a swell guy. He insisted on paying our tuition. So we don't have to go to public school. I'd better think up more tall tales to tell my old friends.

ᘡᘡᘡᘡᘡᘡᘡᘡᘡᘡ

September 1, 1930
Dear Diary,

Last night, Daddy said, "Things are worse than I've told you." Well, he actually said it to Mother. I was sitting at the top of the stairs. He said when that stupid stock market was going up, up, up, he'd bought stock with all of our savings. His bosses at the bank loved him so much, they let him borrow money to buy even more stock. "It's all gone," he said. "We have nothing left. Worse yet, we owe the money I borrowed."

Today, Reuben ran ahead when Daddy walked us to school. He yelled, "Daddy! There's a long line of people at your bank." Daddy's face turned gray again. He acted so strange. "We're not going out of business," he said, as if he was talking to one of the people in line, as if he was hoping to change his own mind. "You don't have to take all of your money out."

PS: I just figured out how poor we are. We don't even have money in the bank to take out.

September 6, 1930
Dear Diary,

Daddy was fired! He came home early yesterday smiling. I thought he was going to tell us some swell news. But no. He sat all of us down in the living room and said the bank had to let him go. He is now officially unemployed. He promised he would find a new job right away.

PS: He also said we were rich, and someday

we'd have money again. How can that be?

PSS: That gold coin sure would come in handy. Why'd you have to hide it so well, Dolly?

September 8, 1930
Dear Diary,

After school, Reuben and I overheard Mother laughing and talking to someone. "I simply can't believe it," she said. "My husband, the wealthy investment banker, must have forgotten to send you that check. I'll make sure it goes out today." When we got to the kitchen, we found her laughing into the phone. Daddy was at the table. His eyes were red.

P.S. I've never seen Daddy cry before.

September 15, 1930
Dear Diary,

I don't want to be in the living room

anymore. It's crowded with people and I hate all of them. Mother says we have to "sit Shiva," for a week. Well I don't care if that's what Jewish people do when someone dies. A whole week of this? Everybody is out there laughing and eating and drinking. Mother goes from crying all the time to acting like everything is normal. She'll say things like, "You have to face life." Why should I want to?

PS: Mother looks so old all of a sudden.

PPS: My daddy is dead.

<hr>

September 16, 1930
Dear Diary,

Mr. Dan brought by a huge platter of wonderful cookies for Reuben and me today. He sat us down on the couch and got on his knees in front of us. "Your daddy was such a good man," he said. "His heart could not withstand how cruel life can be." Then he told us a bunch of funny stories about Daddy.

After he left, Reuben and I went back to my room. Guess what? It felt better to laugh a little. Also some friends came over after school to "pay their respects."

PS: I wish everyone would just leave us alone. Mostly I just want to cry.

◠◠◠◠◠◠◠◠◠◠

September 17, 1930
Dear Diary,

Now everyone at school knows we are poor. The kids look at me as if I am a street person. I hate it and I hate them. Today, a man knocked on the door. Mother argued with him. We kneeled on the couch and watched through the window as that awful man loaded our car onto a truck. Reuben whispered to me, "I guess Mother never sent that check." At dinner, Mother told us that Daddy had borrowed from the life insurance policy. She said we have no money but we have each other, and for that we are very rich.

PS: Tell that to the kids at school.

September 18, 1930
Dear Diary,

I went to play the "Bolero" album, but the Victor was gone. So was the radio. Mother sold them to pay the mortgage and buy food. I hid our albums under my bed.

I found Mother crying. "We've lost our house," she said.

PS: It's not fair. My daddy is dead. They've taken our car and our music and now our house. Will they put us out on the street?

September 20, 1930
Dear Diary,

We're moving! Mr. Dan has a farmer friend Leo who could lose his farm if he doesn't get any help. When Mr. Dan told them about us, they said they have a bedroom we could use for free if we would help his wife, Cora. Mother packed one suitcase for each of us and sold the rest of our worldly possessions to a man with a big truck.

We board a train to our new home this afternoon.

PS: I can't believe this, dear diary. We are to become farmers. I can't wait to get away from this horrible city. But farmers? Cows and chickens? Like Old MacDonald? Ugh.

Chapter Five
Home, Home on the Range

۞۞۞۞۞۞۞۞۞۞

NOW: A Farmhouse in Crossroads, Colorado, 1931

Jenny's lids squinted open. When she saw dusty mustard walls, she scrunched them shut again, wanting to go back to her dream where she'd just awoken in her old bed, in her old room, in her old home. Half awake, half asleep, Jenny's dream continued.

The bed is cushiony. "Jenny. Jenny," someone calls. She runs downstairs as Daddy walks out the front door. She catches up to him and looks around. But she is not in New York City. She's on Leo's farm and Cora is warbling, "It's the way of the farm. We've picked the crops. But the fields are too dry. How will we pay? Jenny. . . and Reuben. . . but they'll be homeless."

The rocker's creak and movement startled Jenny's body awake again.

Her diary sat in her lap, opened to the very last entry she'd written. She remembered writing it the day they'd moved to Colorado.

She turned to the first blank page, but the sound of someone slamming the outhouse door caused her to look outside. It was Leo, staring off into the distance. Was he worried about a drought? There hadn't been much rain since she'd been at the farm. A soft tap on the bedroom door startled her. Definitely Cora. It reminded her of Leo and Cora talking the night before. Of hearing her name. Did Leo and Cora want her family to move out? Or had it all been a dream?

Jenny slapped the book closed. Diaries were for children. She was nearly thirteen and working on a farm. She was about to start a new school. She didn't have time for such silliness. Jenny removed the scarf and lamp, opened the box, and placed her diary back inside with the record albums. Then she woke Reuben.

The two pulled on their work clothes, did their chores, and changed into the old clothes their Mother had resewn. Today was their first day of school.

"I'll drop you two off today," Leo said. "Pay close attention, New York Jenny. You'll need to learn the route."

⌒⌒⌒⌒⌒⌒⌒⌒⌒⌒

At lunch, Jenny and Reuben ate together. Reuben looked up from his ham sandwich. "I love my class."

"Oh you do, Mr. Big Man on Campus? Let me guess. You're older than any of the other kids."

Reuben's smile stretched wide. "My teacher said I should have been in your classroom, but it was too crowded. Besides, the principal wanted me separated from you."

"Well, I hate almost everything about this place," Jenny said. "Most of these kids dress like they've come to school right from the fields."

Reuben stopped eating. "I know! Have you ever seen so many pairs of overalls? But you said you hated almost everything, Jenny. What do you like?"

"Well, there's a girl named Fannie who seems all right. At first, I wasn't sure how to take her. When the teacher introduced me as the new student who had traveled all the way from New York City, she reached across the aisle and squeezed my hand. Well, I yanked my hand away."

Reuben made his "I'm puzzled" bunny nose. "Why? She sounds nice."

Jenny took a sip from the small bottle of milk her teacher had given her. "Well, I was so surprised. But she just smiled and said, 'Welcome to Old MacDonald's School of farm kids.' I knew right then and there we'd be good friends."

When the afternoon bell rang, Jenny and Reuben headed home, walking along the dry and dusty road. Reuben counted his steps, but gave up after 500.

"It's just a wee bit less than two miles,"

Leo said at dinner, as he passed the fresh cornbread.

Jenny was quick to complain. "Are we going to have to walk every day?"

"Your legs will grow strong," Mother said. "Now tell me what you've learned today for all that walking."

"About Hoovervilles," Reuben said.

"And boxcar kids," Jenny added.

"Hoovervilles?" Leo sounded surprised. "What'd they tell you in that school about Hoovervilles?"

Reuben stared at his plate and then put his fork down. "Miss Joan, that's my teacher. She said they are shanty towns where people go when they lose their jobs and are kicked out of their homes." Tears welled up in his eyes. "The people live in tents or buildings made out of boxes. They build them on the edges of towns so the rich people don't have to look at them."

Jenny squeezed his hand, wondering if that's where they'd end up someday.

"We have Cora and Leo to thank for

giving us such a fine place to live," Mother said, seeming to read her mind. "And come to think of it, at the store today, some boys not much older than you, Jenny, came in. One was chatting with me while the other two walked around the store shopping. Well, at least I thought they were shopping," she said, wiping her mouth with the cloth napkin. "They ran out. Never paid me a cent for whatever it was they'd picked up! I wonder if they might have been boxcar kids. They looked a bit hungry and lost."

"Maybe so, Mother. From what Miss Nolene said, they ride the trains, looking for work."

"Or great adventures," Leo said, with a far-off stare, smiling. Jenny wondered if he wanted to go on one himself. Her mind wandered, wondering if she could be that brave.

It had been a long day. Reuben and Jenny did their homework, Mother and Cora cleaned up, and Leo headed outside. "More work to do," he said. "I'm guessing some of us wouldn't take too kindly to becoming boxcar kids." Cora frowned, then let out the strangest chuckle Jenny had ever heard.

It was Jenny's turn to make the bread. As she kneaded the dough, she imagined riding on a train. Could they go anywhere they wanted? Later, she fell into a deep sleep, dreaming she'd boarded a train, dressed as a boy. She was riding the rails to find her gold coin. The only person who could help her was Dolly.

When the rooster crowed again, she could barely move. That long walk home from school along with her other chores had been too much. But Cora was at their door. "Rise and shine, children. It's late and you have work to do before school. Hurry up and Leo will drive you."

At school, Fannie was waiting outside the building. "Hello city girl! Who's your sidekick?"

Reuben looked up at Jenny, as if he were not sure how to take this girl's comment. Jenny laughed. "Farmer Fannie," she said, "meet my little brother, Reuben."

Fannie examined Reuben, then said, "Since you weren't in our class yesterday, I guess they dumped you in the nursery school room."

"But I'm not—"

"Clearly a mistake," Fannie said, interrupting him. "You look much too old and dashing to be in there."

Reuben's cheeks flushed. He turned and ran into the building. But in that one sentence, Jenny was certain Fannie had won him over.

On the way to their classroom, Jenny whispered, "Remind me to tell you about my dream last night."

At lunch, Jennie shared her dream along with a few small tales: Her daddy was a successful banker. He worked in New York. Leo and Cora were family friends and needed help on their farm. So she, her brother, and mother moved to Colorado to help out for a little while.

Fannie told Jenny her story, how her mother had died when she was born. Her father had lost his business in the city. Her older brother had to quit school to help their father. And the three of them lived in a small outbuilding on a farm not far from Leo and Cora's. "But we're pretty good now," she said. "You know. We've got each other."

Listening to Fannie's history surprised Jenny, releasing a well of emotion that sent tears streaming down her cheeks.

"Jenny! I'm sorry," Fannie said, pulling a handkerchief out of her bag. "Did I say something wrong?"

Jenny wiped her eyes. "No. I did." She fessed up about her old life, how they'd lost everything, and how life broke Daddy's heart. She even told her about Dolly and their magical gold coin.

It felt good to let it all out, but she didn't want Fannie's pity. She wiped her eyes again and said, "Guess what? My mother saw some boxcar kids at Mr. Hilbig's store. Want to go to the train station after school some day and see what they're like?"

"I don't know. Maybe. But why?"

"Come on, Fannie, just to see if they're there. The truth is, I'm starting to worry about what'll happen if Leo and Cora can't afford to let us stay with them anymore. I want to know what other people do. I sure as heck wouldn't want to live in a Hooverville."

"What about your brother?"

"I'll tell my mother I've been invited to your house and she'll pick him up. You can tell your dad that you've been invited to mine."

"How will you get home?"

"We'll walk. It's a long way, but not a big deal."

"No kidding, Farmer Jenny. I do it every day."

☙☙☙☙☙☙☙☙☙☙

Later that week, they put their plan into action. When Mother arrived at school in Leo's truck to pick up Jenny and Reuben, Jenny grabbed Fannie's hand and pulled her over. "Mother, I want you to meet my new friend. Mother. Fannie. Fannie. Mother."

"Very nice to meet you Mrs. Gold," Fannie said. "It's nice to meet other city folk out here in the sticks."

Mother laughed. The two talked for a bit until Jenny interrupted. "Mother, Miss Nolene asked if Fannie and I could help her today and clean the erasers and chalkboards. Is that all right?" She'd told so many lies over the previous year but this time, her throat tightened up a little. She added, "Fannie doesn't live far from us and we can walk home."

"All right, dear. You'll still have time to do your homework and help with dinner." And with that, she drove off with Reuben waving wildly at Fannie. As soon as they were out of sight, Jenny and Fannie ran in the opposite direction toward town and the train station.

Jenny remembered thinking how cute the rural station had seemed when they'd first arrived. Hardly as grand as Penn Station in New York. "Oh Fannie, you should see the enormous rooms and arched ceilings there. There's even bronze sculptures."

"What's the matter, Farmer Jenny? Aren't our one-room building and two railroad tracks good enough for you?"

The two laughed and ran the rest of the way. As the building came into view, the girls could see people sitting in the grass outside. So they crept closer.

"That boy looks like he could be Reuben's age," Fannie said 'And the one standing by the building reminds me of Joseph in our class. They're our age!"

"Fannie," Jenny whispered. "I need you to get me a pair of your brother's overalls, a shirt, and a hat to wear."

Fannie's head spun back to look at the boys, then returned to Jenny, then back to the boys again. "You're going to become a boxcar kid?"

"No, silly. I just want to talk to them. It'll be easier if I look like them."

Fannie laughed. "Jenny Gold. Riding the rails. That'll be the day, city girl."

Chapter Six
Can't You Hear the Whistle Blowing

After school, Jenny hid Fannie's yellow and blue flowered sack behind the outhouse. Inside, were a pair of her older brother's overalls, his long-sleeved denim shirt, an old jacket, cap, and old shoes.

At dinner, Leo announced that he'd sold a cow to cover this month's mortgage payment on the farm. Mother didn't have any better news. Mr. Hilbig gave away some of her hours to two more women whose husbands had lost their jobs.

"Well, everyone around here is going to have to work harder," Cora warbled. "We'll get by. Remember what they say. 'Repair, reuse, make do, and don't throw anything away.'"

Jenny rolled her eyes. She already had to clean out the chicken coop, milk the cows, and gather eggs. Sometimes she had to walk miles to and from school, then do her homework, help wash clothes, fix dinner, and bake bread. Her clothes had been let out and re-hemmed. And Cora was showing Mother how to make clothes from flour sacks. How much more could she stand?

"But Mr. Hilbig made me a promise," Cora added. "He'll try to sell whatever we bake in his store. Jenny, you and your mother and I will be baking every night."

Cora brought out an enormous bowl for the flour, yeast, and water. They took turns kneading a huge amount of dough. After they let the dough rise, Jenny made round loaves, patting pieces of dough into circles. All the while, she fantasized about being a boxcar kid.

Dressed like a boy, she slips into the group of boys waiting in the grass. They hoot and holler and shake her hand. Warmed by the sun, they share stories about where they've gone, how they live. As the boys hop on board, she slips away, changes her clothes, and is doing her morning chores.

While she waited for the loaves to rise before baking them, she formed a plan. One train passed through the station every day, arriving at night, leaving just before dawn. She'd walk there long before dawn, talk to some of the boxcar kids, and make it back home before Cora tapped on her door.

∩∩∩∩∩∩∩∩∩∩

Hours before dawn, Jenny gently eased herself out of bed. In silence, she dressed to do her chores.She tiptoed into the kitchen and stuffed a fresh loaf of bread in her book bag. Outside, she went immediately to the outhouse, changed into the clothes hidden behind the bushes, and rushed off toward town.

What she hadn't considered was how inky dark and chilly it would be in the middle of the night. Fortunately, the path to the station was a straight shot. She walked quickly. Soon enough, the sound of a car motor grew louder. She turned toward the sound, to the headlights coming her way, then turned back and kept walking, nearly running, praying it would just pass her by. The vehicle reached her, slowed, and then stopped just ahead of her.

The words "Refresh yourself. Drink Coca Cola," were painted on the red wooden-panel truck. She should have felt relieved since she'd forgotten to bring anything to drink. Only her whole body began to shake. A man stuck his head out of the window. "Need a lift, son?"

Jenny quickly turned to see with whom the man was speaking. *Had a boy been following her?* Then it hit her. Her clothes. Stuffing her hair under the cap. It had worked. "No sir," she said, lowering her voice a bit. "I like walking the roads this time of night."

"Suit yourself," said the man.

"But I sure could use one of them there Coca Colas," Jenny said, purposefully changing her grammar. "Only I got no money."

"Where you headed?" the man asked.

"Wherever the train is headed, sir," Jenny

replied.

The man shook his head and turned as if he were going to drive away. But then he stuck his hand out the window, holding a bottle. "Here you go, son."

Jenny took the bottle. The man closed the window and drove off. She bit her lip each time another vehicle passed. None stopped.

Walking as fast as she could, Jenny soon arrived at the desolate-looking train station. The grounds were deserted. Where were all the kids? Had she picked the wrong day? Had they already jumped aboard a car?

A whistle blew and the train wheels began to turn. She'd come so far but hadn't learned anything about what it was like to be a boxcar kid. Then a head popped out from one of the cars farther back. A boy, maybe a couple years older, waved at her. His clothes looked so much like hers, she could have been looking in the mirror, except that he was much taller and very handsome.

"Grab my hand," he yelled.

Jenny panicked. She'd never meant to

actually get on the train. The whistle blew again. She yelled, "Nah, changed my mind."

"I can't hear you!" the boy yelled back. As the boxcar crept by her, he reached out and grabbed her arm. Jenny tried to pull away from his tight grip. But the boy was too strong, forcing her to run alongside. The next thing she knew, he'd pulled her into the car. Another boy had grabbed her legs to make sure they were inside.

"Phew. You made it," said the first boy. "Almost didn't get you aboard."

Jenny's heart chugged faster than the train. She looked out the open doors. She would have to jump out to get home before the rooster crowed. Only the train had picked up speed, moving faster and faster.

Tears swamped her eyes. There was no getting off. She quickly wiped them away, remembering she was supposed to be a boy.

"Did you see that, Howie?" said the first boy. "He's crying!"

The boy who'd grabbed her legs moved behind her. "'Fraid not, Donald. I didn't see nothing." Then he yanked off Jenny's cap, her hair falling to her shoulders. "But now I do. Like I expected. He's a girly girl."

"Oh who cares," Jenny blurted out, suddenly frightened, her heart slamming in her chest. "I . . . I can give you bread and cola."

Donald said, "Well, surely, Miss, um, Miss . . ."

"Jenny," she replied. "Any idea how far it is to the next station?"

"I'm not positive. But I guess about an hour," said Howie, popping her cap in the air with his fists. "And we're starving. Did you say bread and cola? Is that all you got?"

The three settled on the floor at one end of the boxcar. Jenny divvied up the bread, trying to hide her shaking hands. She'd gotten herself into such a mess, alone on a train with two strange boys, racing away from Leo's farm. But she refused to show her fear. So she told them a few tall tales.

"I started riding the rails way back in New York," she said, spitting out her words like bullets between bites of bread. "My father is a big banker in the city. But when people lost their money, he started giving all of our things to them. You know, charity cases."

Howie yanked on her arm. "Give me some more bread," he said.

Donald pushed him away. "Let her be!"

Jenny pulled another small piece of bread off for each boy. "Well, I don't like people feeling sorry for me, you see. So I didn't want to do that to them. And I didn't like giving them all of my stuff. So I ran away to get a job."

"Well at least your dad has a job," Howie said. "Mine got arrested for breaking and entering. My mother drinks whiskey day and night. Heck, they couldn't remember they had a son most of the time."

"That's awful," Jenny said, hoping this boy would leave her alone. "What about you?" she asked Donald.

"My father sent me away. Long story. Anyway, a friend told me there's a mine west of Grand Junction that's hiring."

"Is that your luggage?" Jenny asked, looking at the black satin satchel he'd set next to him.

"Yep. Brought a sleeping bag, a few pairs of socks, undershorts, and stuff. You might call it all my worldly possessions." Donald shoved his satchel and laughed. Jenny laughed too. Howie had curled up and fallen asleep.

"I wouldn't be so tough on the people who want to help each other," Donald added. "Being charitable and all."

Jenny looked at her bottle of cola, wondering how she'd get the metal top off. "Charity? Why shouldn't I," she said. "They just look down on me and feel sorry for me." The truth slipped out before she could stop it.

Donald just nodded his head like he understood. Then he took the bottle from her, set it at an angle to a ledge on the side of the boxcar, and smacked it with his fist. The cap popped off. "Here you go. That's not what charity means, by the way."

Jenny took a swig of the cola and passed it

back to Donald. Her worries about getting in trouble back at the farm were overtaking her fear of this boy. And she didn't want to talk anymore about charity, so she changed the subject. "Why'd your dad send you away?"

He stared off for a while. "The doctors said my mother had something called psychosis. My dad made a decent living—he was the principal at a school—but it cost him a lot to put her in a good hospital. Then everyone started losing their jobs. To get Dad's mind off things, he and I would go door to door, seeing what our friends needed. If we had it, we'd give it to them. Clothes. Food. And the like.

"Then the town closed Dad's school. He didn't have enough money to take care of my mom and raise me. Those neighbors we'd given things to, they came by to help us out. It got us by for a while. But eventually Dad had to move Mom into a different hospital. A horrible place. He got all depressed. Said I'd be better off if he sent me out in the world. Can you believe that? My dad, the school principal, said I should quit school and get a job. He found his old sleeping bag, packed it in Ma's old silk satchel, gave me a necklace of hers to sell, and kicked me out."

Jenny had thought Howie's story was sad. But now tears were streaming down her cheeks. "You are so brave. I'm nothing but a liar. My daddy isn't in New York. He's dead. We used to be rich, but we lost everything. Helping on Leo and Cora's farm gave us a place to live."

"Why all the tall tales, Miss Jenny?"

"The truth always seems harder to face than all my lies. Then the lies get harder to keep up with. But if you must know, you guys frightened me."

Donald smiled. "Glad our stories helped you find your truth."

"The truth? I hate living on a farm. I never meant to get on board this train. I just wanted to find out what it'd be like to ride the rails. In case . . . in case we have nowhere else to go. Donald's yawn interrupted her. "Sorry. I guess I'm putting you to sleep."

"No, I'm sorry, Miss Jenny. Howie and I were kicked off a train at the station before yours. A railroad cop said he'd arrest us the next time we trespassed on railroad property. So we walked the tracks to your station." Then Donald closed his eyes and went to sleep.

Jenny moved closer to the door and watched the train move away from the rising sun peeking over the horizon. The rooster had surely crowed by now. The family was up. And there was no getting home to do her chores. Jenny's eyes grew heavy. Behind her closed lids, all she could see were Leo and Cora's angry faces. Not to mention her mother's angry face for upsetting Cora and Leo. She'd get to the next station and hop on a train heading back . . .

"Jenny Gold."

Jenny's eyes popped open. Donald stood over her. "Hey Miss Jenny. I think someone might be looking for you."

Jenny rubbed her eyes with her palms, rattled by her strange surroundings. The train had stopped moving. A man she recognized—the only farmhand left at Leo's—stuck his head in the boxcar. "Boys, don't mean to give you any trouble. Just looking for a girl. Well, I'll be." He looked away and yelled, "You were right, Mr. Leo! She's in here."

The next thing Jenny knew, Leo was at the door. "Bust my britches. Dressed like a boy. Are you all right?"

Donald had jumped off the train. He turned to help Jenny get down.

"Leo, how did you find—I never meant to—"

Leo moved between her and Donald, giving her his hand. "Jump, New York Jenny. Let's get you back to the farm. Your mother and Cora are very upset."

"I'm so sorry, Leo." She turned to Donald. "I know you meant well pulling me on board. Good luck with the job hunting. Oh, and here's the rest of the bread for you and Howie."

"That's right charitable of you, Miss Jenny."

His words stopped her. "You said I had it

wrong about what charity means. How so?"

"Just something my dad taught me. Charity comes from a Latin word that means preciousness. That Latin word came to mean an unconditional love for others, Miss Jenny. People just show it in different ways."

"We can talk about this later, but know you are one lucky lady, my finding you just now," Leo said on the way back to the farm. "That train was about to head out again for a long stretch. I'd have never caught up to you."

"How did you know where to look for me?"

Leo went on to explain how everyone thought she'd been outside doing her chores. When it was clear she was gone, Mother called Fannie to see if she knew anything. Fannie fessed up about the boxcar plans.

"When you weren't at our train station, I figured I'd try to catch up to the next stop."

"I know I'm in big trouble, Leo. But I

never meant to get on the train with those boxcar boys. I just wanted to learn about them to see if someday I could do it."

"What's the matter, New York Jenny? Life too hard for you on the farm?"

Leo's words settled on Jenny like a bowl of smashed eggs. Donald and Howie's lives were hard. At least she had a bed and a mother and brother who loved her and lots of good food.

As Leo's truck rumbled up the farm's dirt road, the wind kicked up surrounding them in a cloud of dust. As it settled, the front door flew open. Reuben burst outside, running down the path. When the truck came to a stop, Jenny got out and ran to meet. All the while, she looked up toward her mother standing on the porch.

The swelling in her mother's eyes opened Jenny's eyes. She'd been so worried about getting in trouble for being late for her chores. She didn't stop to think that anyone might be worried about her.

"Jenny!" cried Reuben, nearly tackling

her with a hug, tears rolling down his cheeks. "After everything we've lost, I thought you were gone, too."

Chapter Seven
Brother Can You Spare Me a Dime

"I'm so sorry," Jenny said over a huge breakfast of biscuits, fresh jam, eggs, and ham. "I truly thought I'd make it home before the sun rose."

"You are important here, Jenny," Cora said. "Reuben and I had to tend the cows and chickens without you this morning."

Jenny looked around the table. At Leo and Cora who gave her a bedroom and food and needed her help. At her mother and brother who loved her so much. Could she possibly be feeling lucky to be a farmer, sitting there with her new family?

Leo dropped Jenny and Reuben at school. Moments later, Fannie ran out of the building and up to the truck. "Please don't hate me," she said.

Jenny smiled. "Hate you? Why you're my

lucky charm." Then she turned to Leo. "See you after school." She headed to the building, but then turned and said, "You know, I was pretty darn lucky that you found me. But I was even luckier I got myself into that mess. It helped me figure out who I am."

"It did, did it? Well, see you after school, New York Jenny," Leo said.

She walked back to the truck and whispered, "My friends call me Farmer Jenny."

⌒⌒⌒⌒⌒⌒⌒⌒⌒⌒

At lunch, Jenny filled Fannie in on Donald, Howie, and her adventure. Fannie listened, asked the right questions, but had her own story to tell. The Martins, who owned the farm where her family lived, might have to sell their place.

"It's this stupid depression. And the drought keeps getting worse. Mr. Martin said the only thing he can grow are weeds and grasshoppers!"

An idea began to form in Jenny's mind.

"I want to do something to help them," added Fannie. "But I don't know what it could be."

"I do, Fannie!" Jenny blurted out, remembering her talk with Donald.

"Another idea, New York Jenny? Didn't the last one teach you anything?"

"You'll like this one. Tonight, go home and make a list of all the things your family and the owners need right now. Try to be specific. Then make a second list. And this is the important one. Go through all your stuff, anything on the farm that you have that you can give away."

"Why?"

"You and I are going to be the Robin Hoods of the West. We'll take from those who have and give to those who don't—only we won't steal."

For an hour after school a couple days a week, Jenny, Reuben, and Fannie went door to door, explaining their plan. Soon enough, neighbors and town folk gave them their lists.

When Jenny told Cora about her plan, she said, "Like I once told you. It's the way of the farm." Cora took Jenny's face in her hands, touching her for the first time since she'd moved there. "Now you really ARE part of it. You've come a long way."

Cora told Jenny to clear away an area in the barn to use as a staging ground for the items they collect. She even offered to drive the truck for pickups and deliveries.

With the help of Reuben and Cora, Jenny and Fannie collected tools and clothes and food and all kinds of things their neighbors and townsfolk had to give away. Reuben showed great skill at sorting and inventorying items. Sometimes Cora drove; sometimes Mother, sometimes Leo. Soon enough, they began to fill the needs of their neighbors with the items they'd collected.

Jenny never knew how hard she could work or how good she could feel having a purpose. She gave away her old dresses, her Tiddlywinks, and her jacks and ball to a girl on another farm. Cora offered half of the bread they baked to share with others. Reuben couldn't bear to give away his Spirit of St. Louis but he donated his Lincoln Logs.

It was a Saturday when the weather grew colder. Mother unpacked the jacket Jenny wore the previous winter in New York. Staring in the mirror, Jenny pushed her hands in the pockets to stretch it out as much as she could. Her right hand hit something hard. And round. And flat.

A coin.

She pulled it out, but in her excitement dropped it on the floor. Just as her mother walked in.

"My goodness! That's the gold coin Daddy gave you when you were born!"

"Gave me?" Jenny told her the real tale about finding it and the hide and seek game she and Dolly played. "I'm sure you'll find a good use for this," she said, feeling happy to give something to her mother.

"We were going to give it to you on your sixteenth birthday, but I lost it so many years ago. It's yours, my darling. Daddy would want you to buy something special for yourself."

Jenny stared out the window to the dry fields. Over the past few weeks, she'd filled her own list. Flour sack cloth, jam, pickled vegetables and spices for Cora. A part that she'd found for Leo's tractor. But there had been two items on her list that had been impossible to fill.

⌒⌒⌒⌒⌒⌒⌒⌒⌒⌒

Since riding the rails with the boxcar boys, Jenny had promised herself that she wouldn't lie anymore. But when Mother picked her and Reuben up the next afternoon to work on "Operation Robin Hood," Jenny told one last small tale.

"I can't work today, Mother," she said.

"My teacher said I have to stay and get some help on my math." When Mother drove off, Jenny headed toward town.

Chapter Eight
Happy Days Are Here Again!

⌒⌒⌒⌒⌒⌒⌒⌒⌒⌒⌒

At dinner the next night, Jenny could barely contain her excitement. She finally understood why Daddy preferred to give away presents rather than get them. When it was time to clear away the dishes, she said, "Cora, could we all sit here for a few more minutes? I have a surprise for you."

Cora smiled, but said, "Only a few, Jenny. Lots of work still to do."

Jenny ran outside and found the truck waiting. She'd prearranged for the store owner to deliver what she'd purchased at sunset. The man lifted a crate out of the back of his truck and brought it inside the kitchen. Then he went back outside. A few minutes later, he delivered a second crate. "That should do it, Miss Jenny. These are tough times for my business. My family thanks you."

Reuben jumped up from the table. "What are these, Jenny?"

"Leo, Cora, this one is for you." She pointed to the smaller of the two crates.

"Well bust my britches," Leo said as he lifted the top off the crate. "A radio! Help me with this, Jenny."

Jenny took the radio from him, set it on the kitchen counter, and turned it on. "It runs on batteries, Leo." A shooshing sound filled the room. "Static," she said. She turned the knob left, then right until she found a station—the only station they could get. "I guess we're going to have to trade someone for an antenna," Jenny said.

But from that one station, the sound of a woman's voice filled the room. "When the moon comes over the mountain . . ."

"Why, that's Kate Smith," Mother said. "Your daddy and I heard her in New York on Broadway years ago."

Cora closed her eyes as she listened. When she finally opened them, she said, "That's kindly of you, Jenny. You must have made a tremendous trade."

"Nope. Mother will explain it later. Mother, Reuben, it's your turn. Open the other box!"

Mother helped Reuben lift the lid of the much larger box. Mother gasped.

"It's a Victrola," yelled Reuben. "I can't believe it's a Victrola!"

⌒⌒⌒⌒⌒⌒⌒⌒⌒⌒

The next day was Saturday. Reuben and Jenny did their chores. Cora fixed a breakfast of baked goods and jam their appreciative neighbors traded, and the eggs offered up by their own chickens.

Afterward, Jenny whispered something to Mother who said, "Go ahead, my darling. I'll help Cora. You get it all set up."

Jenny retrieved the record albums from the treasure box and brought them to the living room. She placed the first album on the Victrola platter, turned the wind-up arm to get the platter spinning, placed the needle on the record, and danced back to the kitchen to the tune of "Happy Days Are Here Again."

"You've come a long way, New York—I mean Farmer Jenny," Leo said, as he headed out the door. Then he stopped, turned around, and smacked the door jam. "But that music makes me happy there is still a piece of New York left in you. With all the hard work you've done, I say we all take the morning off."

"I hope you'll like my favorite," she said, waving everyone into the living room.

The drum beat began its repeated rhythm and the lulling sound of the first instrument floated through the room. Reuben's smile infected everyone. He pretended to be a conductor, and pointed his make-believe baton at Jenny. "What is it?" he called.

"Flute," she said. Tears flooded Mother's eyes from the sweet memories. Leo's head moved back and forth to the beat of the drum, and Cora closed her eyes and smiled.

When a new instrument began to repeat the exotic music, Reuben would point his baton at Jenny and ask, "What is it?"

Jenny felt a sweet sadness, remembering the game she'd played with Daddy, correctly naming each new sound. "Flute . . . Clarinet... Bassoon . . . ."

When the French horns began to play, Reuben asked, "What is it?"

But something out the window distracted Jenny. Her smile disappeared as her attention divided between the music's lulling sounds and what her eyes were seeing but couldn't understand. Reuben tapped her with his make-believe baton, and teased, "Come on, Jenny. Don't you know what it is?"

"French horns, silly!" she said. The sky had divided as well. To the south of the barn, golden sunny skies appeared as calm and peaceful as Ravel's "Bolero." But to the north, a dark cloud, more like a curtain of black dust, boiled up from the ground to a thousand feet or more into the sky. The onslaught of wind and dirt whipped up branches and paper. Overwhelmed by what looked like an enormous rolling wall of dust, even the birds were whirled in the wind.

Reuben was more interested in the return of the oboes and the game he was playing with his sister. "What is it, Jenny?" he asked.

The darkness heading toward the farm sent chills up Jenny's neck. Gravel splattered against the windows and pounded on the roof, accompanying the drum beat. The roof shook, the rafters creaked, and the lights went out.

She peered out of the window at the dust storm enveloping the farm. It differed from the sights and sounds of stormy skies she used to hide from in New York. "I don't know, Reuben," she said. "But let's find out!"

The Stock Market Crash of 1929 and the Beginning of the Great Depression

Imagine American life during the Roaring Twenties as a rising roller-coaster car. Optimistic investors poured money into the stock market. Banks made it easy for their customers to get loans. Investors borrowed money and invested more. Businesses expanded and people moved to the rapidly growing cities. At the same time, farmers were growing concerned. They'd overproduced their crops and could not sell them.

In 1929, the roller-coaster neared its pinnacle. By March, a series of events pushed it over the top. The Federal Reserve warned that people were getting too risky with their investments. Some investors pulled out their money, causing a mini-crash. Then, on October 24, 1929, panicked investors pulled out so much money from the market, it became known as "Black Thursday." Five days later, a greater crash occurred on "Black Tuesday." Stock prices fell. Companies struggled. They had to lay off employees. Those who were laid off struggled too. They pulled their money out of the banks and the stock market to pay bills and provide food for their families.

From 1929 through most of the 1930s, more than fifteen million Americans were out of work, businesses were unable to sell their products, and farmers, who were already feeling the pain of too many crops without enough buyers, found their situation worsening. Many families lost their homes and stood in line for food. Some lived in shanty towns on the outskirts of cities called Hoovervilles. Others jumped aboard trains to seek their fortunes. The youngest of these people were called boxcar kids. In 1932,

Franklin D. Roosevelt won the election against Herbert Hoover. He instituted "New Deal" programs that created jobs and economic growth. The roller-coaster car reached the bottom and could begin to slowly ascend again.

Q & A
with Sue LaNeve

1. What inspired this book?

I wanted to explore what it might be like for a happy and very wealthy family to lose everything during the stock market crash.

2. How did you come up with your character Jenny?

I closed my eyes and tried to imagine how a girl living in 1929 might look and sound. I wanted her to be fun and strong but also confused and struggling.

3. **What are the most interesting things you've learned?**

That yoyos were invented during this era and that dresses were made from flour sacks surprised me! Also, that "Old MacDonald Had a Farm" came out long before this story.

About the Author

The only thing Ms. LaNeve likes more than writing children's books is living aboard her trawler, *m/v Freebird*, cruising the ocean, and watching dolphins swim alongside. She holds an MFA from The Vermont College of Fine Arts and is a Merchant Marine Captain.

Websites to Visit

www.fun-facts.org.uk/america/
   great-depression.htm
http://erroluys.com/
   hobolettersfromridingtherails.htm
http://facts.randomhistory.com/2009/04/
   12_great-depression.html

Writing Prompt

   "New York" Jenny had a hard time adjusting to life on the farm. If you found yourself in her shoes, what would a day on the farm be like for you? Write about why you'd rather be "New York Jenny", "Farmer Jenny," or a little bit of both.